Little Shaq
Takes a Chance

Books by Shaquille O'Neal and illustrated by Theodore Taylor III

Little Shaq
Little Shaq Takes a Chance
Little Shaq: Star of the Week

Little Shaq
Takes a Chance

SHAQUILLE
O'NEAL

illustrated by
Theodore Taylor III

BLOOMSBURY
NEW YORK LONDON OXFORD NEW DELHI SYDNEY

To Uncle Mike, Uncle Jerome, and Aunt Cynthia
for always inspiring me to be the best that I can be
—Shaquille

To my wife, Sarah, and my son, Theo
—Theodore

First published in the United States of America in April 2016
by Bloomsbury Children's Books
Paperback edition published in April 2017
www.bloomsbury.com

Bloomsbury is a registered trademark of Bloomsbury Publishing Plc

For information about permission to reproduce selections from this book, write to
Permissions, Bloomsbury Children's Books, 1385 Broadway, New York, New York 10018
Bloomsbury books may be purchased for business or promotional use. For information on bulk
purchases please contact Macmillan Corporate and Premium Sales Department at
specialmarkets@macmillan.com

Library of Congress has cataloged the hardcover edition as follows:
O'Neal, Shaquille.
Little Shaq takes a chance / by Shaquille O'Neal ; illustrated by Theodore Taylor III.
pages   cm
Summary: Little Shaq doesn't love trying new things, especially if he might not be very
good at them. So when his class is assigned projects for the school's upcoming art show,
he's not sure that his skills will transfer from the basketball court to the art studio. Can
Little Shaq find the confidence to embrace his own style and create a piece for the show?
ISBN 978-1-61963-844-0 (hardcover)
ISBN 978-1-61963-877-8 (e-book) • ISBN 978-1-61963-968-3 (e-PDF)
1. O'Neal, Shaquille—Childhood and youth—Fiction. [1. O'Neal, Shaquille—Childhood and
youth—Fiction. 2. Art—Fiction. 3. Ability—Fiction. 4. African Americans—Fiction.]
I. Taylor, Theodore, III, illustrator. II. Title.
PZ7.O549Ll 2016   [Fic]—dc23   2015010334

ISBN 978-1-61963-878-5 (paperback)

Art created digitally
Typeset in Chaparral, Housearama Kingpin, and Shag Expert Lounge • Book design by John Candell
Printed in China by C&C Offset Printing Co., Ltd., Shenzhen, Guangdong
1 3 5 7 9 10 8 6 4 2

All papers used by Bloomsbury Publishing, Inc., are natural, recyclable products
made from wood grown in well-managed forests. The manufacturing processes
conform to the environmental regulations of the country of origin.

Table of Contents

Chapter 1
PICK AND ROLL

Little Shaq and his cousin Barry pushed open the front door of Little Shaq's house.

"Hi, Mom!" Little Shaq called as they ran into the kitchen.

"Hi, boys," said Mom. "How was the game?"

Little Shaq and Barry had spent the afternoon at the rec center, where they played basketball after school.

"It was great," Little Shaq said. "I scored my first three-point shot!"

"Wow!" said Mom, pulling him in for a hug. "I'm so proud of you."

"It was awesome," said Barry. "Even the other team cheered!"

Little Shaq smiled and opened the refrigerator.

"Now, don't start filling up on

snacks," said Mom. "You need to

save room for dinner."

"But I'm starving!" Little Shaq

whined. "That three-pointer made me hungry."

"How about some grapes?" she said. "Then you boys need to wash up. We have company coming over. I made something special for dinner."

Little Shaq's eyes lit up. He wondered what it could be.

Maybe Mom made pizza with lots of

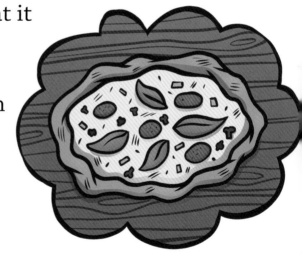

cheese and toppings. Or maybe it was her famous fried chicken and creamy mashed potatoes! Little Shaq sniffed the air for a clue, but he couldn't smell a thing.

Suddenly, Little Shaq's stomach made a loud gurgling noise. He laughed. "I can't wait for dinner."

"Me neither," said Barry. "Pass the grapes!"

"Open up, Barry!" said Little
Shaq. He tossed a grape into Barry's
mouth.

"Three points!" cried Barry. "Now
let me try!"

"Okay, boys, move it along," said Mom. "This is a kitchen, not the rec center."

Little Shaq carefully slid the bowl of grapes across the counter to Barry.

"Hey, what's that?" Barry asked. He pointed to an orange piece of paper that had been under the bowl.

Little Shaq picked up the flier.

"It's for your art show on Friday," said Mom.

"Oh, do we *have* to go to that?" asked Little Shaq.

"Of course!" said Mom. "Have you started your projects yet?"

Parkview Elementary Spring Art Show
Friday 6 p.m.
Rec Center

Contact Ms. Terpenny to volunteer for refreshments

Little Shaq and Barry shook their heads no.

"We're starting tomorrow," said Barry. "I thought I'd try painting."

"That's great, Barry!" said Mom. "What about you, Little Shaq?"

"I don't know," he said. "I'm no good at art."

"You've never given art a real chance. You can do *anything*," said Mom.

Just then the doorbell rang. "We'll talk more about this later," she said. "Go wash up."

Little Shaq and Barry washed their hands and put on clean T-shirts.

When they came downstairs, Malia, Little Shaq's older sister, was setting the final plate on the dining room table. Their younger brother, Tater, followed, adding a napkin to each spot.

Nana Ruth and her friend Mr. Whitten were already sitting.

Mr. Whitten had brought a beautiful bouquet of a dozen pink roses from his garden.

Barry and Little Shaq said hello to Nana Ruth and Mr. Whitten. Then Little Shaq took a seat next to Tater, just as Mom and Dad entered the room.

Mom and Dad were each
carrying a big tray filled with
colorful rolls of rice. Little Shaq was
confused. He had no idea what was
for dinner.

"Oh my. That looks beautiful," said Nana Ruth.

"What *is* it?" asked Little Shaq.

"It's sushi," said Mom. "It's Japanese. I learned how to make it last week."

Little Shaq didn't know what to think. It didn't look like any food he had ever seen before.

"It's raw fish and rice," added Malia.

"What? You mean it's not

cooked?" Little Shaq crinkled his

nose. "No thank you!"

"Oh, Shaquille," said Mom. "Don't

be so stubborn. Try to keep an open mind."

"Your mom worked real hard on this dinner, buddy," Dad said with a nod. "Everyone, please dig in."

Little Shaq watched as the rest of his family piled their plates high with sushi.

Instead of forks, they used two wooden sticks to pick up the rolls. "They're called chopsticks," said Barry. "They're fun."

"*You* eat sushi?" asked Little Shaq.

Barry nodded, swallowing a mouthful. "My favorites are the spicy ones."

"Well, I'm not eating it," Little Shaq said, slumping in his chair. His tummy gurgled again.

This was not the special dinner Little Shaq had hoped for. *At*

least the night can't get any worse,
he thought. But Little Shaq had
thought too soon.

"Mom!" Tater yelled, pushing away
a plate of sushi. "If Little Shaq isn't
eating it, then I'm not either."

Little Shaq could feel his cheeks
get hot. "Tater, stop
copying me!" he shouted.
"Dad!"

"Boys, this
is what's for

dinner," said Dad. "You know the rule."

"If I don't like what's for dinner, I can make something myself," Little Shaq recited.

"That's right," said Mom. "And you can make Tater's dinner too. You know where the peanut butter and jelly are."

Little Shaq slid out of his seat and walked into the kitchen. Tater followed right behind him. Little

Shaq took out a loaf of bread, a jar of crunchy peanut butter, and a jar of grape jelly.

Little Shaq spread peanut butter on one slice of bread and then jelly on another. He squished the two slices together to make a sandwich.

By the time he was done, he had

made two piles of sandwiches—one for him and one for Tater.

"Let's go, Tater," Little Shaq said, handing him a plate of sandwiches. They headed back into the dining room and took their seats.

Little Shaq watched Tater take a big bite of his sandwich. Then he glanced at his own plate. Little Shaq

sighed. He didn't want peanut butter and jelly.

Around the table, everyone seemed to love Mom's dinner. Little Shaq thought he might have been too stubborn after all. The spicy sushi actually sounded pretty good.

But when Little Shaq looked over at the sushi trays, he felt his tummy sink. They were empty.

Chapter 2
IN THE PAINT

At school the next day after recess, Little Shaq's teacher Ms. Terpenny set up two tables of art supplies.

There were watercolor paints, crayons, colored pencils, and markers. She had also laid out paintbrushes, construction paper, and big slabs of clay.

Little Shaq took one look at the art supplies and went straight to his seat.

"Let's get started, class," said Ms. Terpenny. "The art projects you

make this week will be displayed at the rec center as part of the school's spring art show."

The whole room cheered, except for Little Shaq.

"The theme for this year's show is *What We Love*," Ms. Terpenny continued. "So your project should represent something that you care about."

Barry raised his hand. "Can it be about our family?" he asked.

"Absolutely," said Ms. Terpenny.

"What about our pets?" Little Shaq's friend Rosa Lindy asked. Little Shaq listened as his classmates shouted out more questions.

"Okay, settle down," Ms. Terpenny said. "Remember to wait until you're called upon."

Walter Skipple raised his hand.

"Yes, Walter?" she said.

"Does our favorite color count?" he asked.

"Sure!" she said. "Be creative. Now, let's make some art."

Barry quickly grabbed a set of watercolor paints and a paintbrush.

Little Shaq shook his head. Painting seemed hard.

Next to him, Rosa took a pack of

markers and a handful of colored pencils.

Little Shaq shook his head again. He didn't know what to choose.

Then he spied the crayons.

Sometimes Tater made Little Shaq color with him. Little Shaq knew how to use crayons.

He breathed a sigh of relief. Maybe this wouldn't be so bad.

Back at the table, Little Shaq took out an orange crayon and drew a big circle. Then he colored it in.

Rosa leaned over. "I didn't know you loved oranges."

"I don't," said Little Shaq. "It's a *basketball*."

"Oh," said Rosa. "Now I see it."

"Look at mine," said Aubrey Skipple. Walter's twin sister had sketched a picture of their dog, Monty.

"No way!" said Rosa. "I'm doing a portrait of my cat, Mittens."

"This is going to be so great for my newspaper article," said Aubrey.

"Your what?" asked Little Shaq.

"I'm covering the art show for the *Parkview Gazette*," she said.

"My mom is letting me borrow her camera and everything."

Little Shaq glanced down at his

drawing. Rosa was right. It did look like an orange. There was no way his art was good enough for the school newspaper.

Little Shaq crumpled up his drawing and marched back to the supply tables.

"What are you looking for?" Ms. Terpenny asked.

"I don't know," said Little Shaq. "My picture didn't turn out so great."

"Why don't you give the watercolors a shot?" she suggested.

"No thanks," he said. "I don't like painting."

Ms. Terpenny raised her eyebrows. "Have you ever tried it?"

Little Shaq thought for a moment. "No," he admitted.

Ms. Terpenny handed him a set of paints. "If you don't like it, you

can always try something else. Okay?" she said.

Little Shaq nodded.

"Great!" she said. "Let's keep an open mind today."

"That's what my mom always says," he replied.

"She's a smart lady," said Ms. Terpenny.

Little Shaq filled a plastic cup with water and started mixing the colors.

"Want any help?" asked Rosa.

"Sure," he said. "I don't really know what to do."

"Here, let's practice together," Rosa replied.

Rosa dipped a paintbrush into the purple paint and swirled the brush on the paper. She painted three

squiggly lines. "Now, you try," she
said.

Little Shaq gulped and picked up
the paintbrush. He tried to do what
Rosa had just showed him. "First dip

the paintbrush, then squiggle," he said quietly.

Little Shaq painted three more lines on the paper.

"There, you got the hang of it," said Rosa.

Little Shaq smiled and went to work.

Using the black paint, he drew a large rectangle. Then he added a smaller rectangle inside.

"It's a backboard!" Rosa said.

"Yep! I'm going to call this painting *Slam Dunk*. It's not done yet though," said Little Shaq. "I need to add a rim."

With the orange watercolor paint, Little Shaq made a circle beneath the small rectangle. "Hmmm," he mumbled, "that doesn't look like a rim. It's too flat." Little Shaq sighed and put down his paintbrush.

He glanced over at his friends. Rosa was using markers to make lots

of little dots on the page. And Walter

had painted two large squares in

different shades of red and orange.

Little Shaq never knew his friends

were such good artists. He didn't

think anybody would want to look

at his painting. He put his elbows on the table and buried his head in his hands. The art show was only a few days away. What was Little Shaq going to do?

"Uh, Little Shaq?" said Rosa. "Your painting!"

"Huh?" He looked up.

He had put his elbows right on top of the wet paint.

Little Shaq closed his eyes tight. His painting was ruined.

"We can fix this," said Rosa.

"Forget it," Little Shaq said, standing up. "I'm not making anything!"

After school Little Shaq went to the rec center. He couldn't wait to play basketball.

At the sound of Coach Mackins's whistle, Little Shaq

ran down the court. "I'm open!" he yelled.

Walter passed him the ball. "Go for three, Little Shaq!"

Little Shaq dribbled the basketball up and down. As he looked at the rim, he thought about his painting. Little Shaq couldn't get art class off his mind.

"Pass it!" shouted Barry.

Little Shaq threw the ball to Barry, who scored an easy layup.

At the next time-out, Little Shaq took a seat on the bench.

Rosa climbed down from the bleachers.

"What's wrong, Little Shaq?" she asked.

"I'm worried about my project for the art show," he told her.

"So you're not a painter," she said. "Big deal."

"Easy for you to say," he replied. "Your project is really good."

"Yours will be too," said Rosa. "Try the clay tomorrow. I bet you're a natural sculptor."

"You really think so?" he asked.

Rosa nodded as Coach Mackins blew the whistle.

The next day, Ms. Terpenny passed out the class's art projects. Little Shaq looked down at his

smeared painting and then up at the

slab of clay. He was ready to give it a

try.

Little Shaq took the clay and

rolled it back and forth in his hands,

making a ball. The clay felt cool and smooth against his fingers.

Suddenly, he had an idea. He didn't just love basketball, he loved *playing* it. Little Shaq knew exactly what he was going to make.

For the rest of the week, Little

Shaq worked on his sculpture every chance he got. At the end of each day, he covered it in cloth so no one could see it.

On Thursday afternoon, Ms. Terpenny asked everyone to turn in their final projects. Little Shaq took a deep breath and handed his in.

"So, was I right about the clay?" asked Rosa.

Little Shaq smiled. "We'll see," he answered.

Chapter 3
GAME TIME

On Friday night, Little Shaq stood
in front of the mirror and let Dad
straighten his tie.

Mom was making the whole family
get dressed up for the art show.
Little Shaq didn't mind though. He
looked good in a tie.

"All right, everybody," said Mom. "Let's go!"

Little Shaq felt his stomach tense. It was game time. Earlier that day he had been excited about the art show, but now he felt nervous.

"What if no one likes my project?" Little Shaq asked.

"I'll like it," said Tater.

"Me too!" said Malia.

Little Shaq smiled.

"We're all going to love it," said Mom, "because we love *you*."

On the way out the door, Mom grabbed a tray wrapped in plastic.

"What's that?" asked Malia.

"Ms. Terpenny heard about my sushi and asked if I'd make some for tonight," she said.

"Cool," said Little Shaq.

Mom raised a surprised eyebrow and closed the door behind them.

At the rec center, a crowd had started to gather. Little Shaq's heart began to beat fast.

The first art project Little Shaq's family saw was Rosa's cat portrait.

"Wow," said Little Shaq. "I can't

ROSA

believe it's made out of tiny little

dots. It's so neat."

"Thanks!" said Rosa.

Next they came to Walter's and

Aubrey's projects. Even though they

WALTER

AUBREY

were twins, their art looked totally different.

"Very impressive," said Mom.

Little Shaq's heart beat faster. So far, everyone's projects were really good.

Then they arrived at Barry's. Nana Ruth and Mr. Whitten were there too. Little Shaq moved to the front of the crowd to get a closer look.

Barry had painted a family portrait. "Hey," said Little Shaq, "there I am! It looks just like me!"

BARRY

"We'll have to start calling you Picasso," Dad said to Barry. "This is excellent!"

Barry smiled with pride.

Little Shaq realized that his project was up next. His heart began to beat even faster!

There was already a group of people in front of it. Little Shaq tried to hear what they were saying.

"How modern!" a man with a mustache said.

"So lifelike," said a woman in a polka-dot dress.

"It really captures the spirit of the game!" said a man wearing a hat.

Little Shaq thought those all sounded like good things.

Little Shaq's family walked over to

his sculpture. It was called *Basketball with Barry*.

Mom gasped. "It's wonderful," she said.

"Yeah," said Barry, "it looks just like me!"

"I think we should keep this one in the gym," said Coach Mackins.

Suddenly, Aubrey ran to Little Shaq's side. "Smile for the school paper!" she said.

Little Shaq gulped, but when he saw everyone smiling, he did too.

After the camera flashed, Aubrey said, "Hey, Barry, can I ask you some questions about your family portrait?"

"Sure thing," said Barry.

Little Shaq turned to Rosa. "Don't you want to say it?"

"Say what?" Rosa asked.

"I told you so," Little Shaq replied.

"No," she said. "I knew all along you'd make something great!"

"Well, thanks," he said. "Even if it does mean that you were right."

Rosa winked and skipped away to find her parents.

All that smiling had made Little Shaq hungry. "Hey, Tater," he said. "Let's check out the snacks."

On a big buffet table were plates of cheese and crackers, veggies and

dip, cookies and fruit, and Mom's
sushi.

The sushi was almost all gone.

Little Shaq picked up a piece of sushi from the tray.

"What are you doing?" asked Tater.

"I thought I'd give it a try," Little Shaq replied.

"Really?" asked Tater.

"Why not?" he said. "I never thought I'd like sculpting, but now you can call me Michelangelo!"

"Who's that?" asked Tater.

Little Shaq popped a piece of sushi

into his mouth and chewed, tilting his head from side to side. "He's a famous sculptor, like me! Yum!" he said. "Spicy!"

The following week Mom and Dad were getting ready to make dinner.

They called Malia, Little Shaq, and
Tater down to the kitchen.

"What are we all in
the mood for?" Mom
asked.

"Grilled cheese,"
said Malia.

"Chicken nuggets,"
said Tater.

"Lasagna," said Dad.

Little Shaq

looked over at the

refrigerator. Mom had taped up his photo from the newspaper. "I don't know," he said. "Let's try something new."

Shaquille O'Neal is the author of the Little Shaq series, a retired basketball legend, a businessman, and an analyst on the Emmy award–winning show *Inside the NBA* on TNT. During his nineteen-year NBA career, O'Neal was a four-time NBA champion, a three-time Finals MVP, and a fifteen-time All-Star, and he was named the 1993 Rookie of the Year. Since his rookie year, he has been an ambassador for the Boys & Girls Clubs of America, a group with which his relationship goes back to his youth in New Jersey. Passionate about education, O'Neal earned his undergraduate degree from LSU, his MBA from University of Phoenix, and a PhD from Barry University.

www.shaq.com
@Shaq

Theodore Taylor III is the illustrator of the Little Shaq series and was awarded the Coretta Scott King/John Steptoe New Talent Award for his first picture book, *When the Beat Was Born*. An artist, a designer, and a photographer, Taylor received his BFA from Virginia Commonwealth University and lives in Washington, DC, with his wife and son.

www.theodore3.com